ALL DEAD MEN

TOM WATTS

Copyright © 2025 by Tom Watts

All rights reserved.

No portion of this book may be reproduced in any form without written permission from the publisher or author, except as permitted by UK copyright law.

To my family, friends, and co-workers across the years who helped support my dream.

1

Charles held his dying teenage daughter across both of his arms and banged on the door with his blood-soaked fist. She was limp and cold, and Charles waited in the beating night rain for the owner of this rural Bed and Breakfast to answer him.

The front door swung open, and an elderly lady wrapped in a purple dressing gown squinted out at him.

"Please, we need your help. She's been stabbed." Charles pleaded.

The old lady flung her door wide, and Charles blustered through the threshold of the entrance into the warm light. He spun left into the living room and placed Penny down on the beige sofa at the fireplace.

Penny looked up at her father through heavy eyelids. Her hands were still clutching at the gored wound in her abdomen. Charles pushed his hands down on it too, to stem the blood. He could smell its strong, metallic tang.

Charles glanced over his shoulder. The elderly lady was standing rigid at the doorway. Her face was white.

"Call the ambulance and get me some towels," Charles barked.

She limped out of the room and called to upstairs. "Harry! We need some towels now!"

Charles peered as the woman hobbled away into her kitchen and out of sight. When he and Penny were alone, Charles left his daughter and crept back into the unoccupied main hallway where he'd rushed in. He saw the Land Rover keys resting in a ceramic dish on the reception table and swiped them.

Dashing back into the living room, he hoisted Penny to her feet and rolled her left arm over his shoulders.

"Come on, Pen," he muttered. "The doctor's office is in the next town."

He supported her waist with his left hand, and together they shuffled out of the building. They left a watery, maroon blood trail on the floorboards.

Charles reached the gravel driveway and rested Penny's back against the side of the vehicle. The rain was pouring, and he fumbled with the keys.

"Oi!" A voice called out from behind him. Charles swung around. The elderly couple were advancing on him from the house. The old man was tall, bald and had the towels gripped in his hand like a fist. "That's ours!" he bellowed.

Before they could get to him, Charles reached behind himself and yanked out the nine-millimetre pistol from his waistband and pointed at the old man's head.

The old man stumbled backwards. He tried to shield his wife with his body.

"Dad... Don't," Penny mumbled. But Charles kept the gun trained on them, as he unlocked and opened the passenger side door with his free hand.

"Why are you doing this?" The old woman blurted. "We're helping you?"

"The ambulance isn't coming." Charles said. He helped Penny lift herself inside and carefully closed the passenger door on her.

"We'll call the police, then! You, animal!" the old man grunted.

With his weapon still aimed at them, Charles moved around to the driver's side of the vehicle. Charles started the engine with a roar and kicked up the gravel as he sped past the old couple and out onto the blackened country road.

He finally caught his breath. In the darkness, Charles glanced down at his daughter in the passenger seat. She was leaking all over the place. He wedged the pistol in between his legs and held her hand.

"It's alright, Pen. I got you," he whispered.

He scanned the rear-view mirror. And then, he saw it.

The glowing wall of gas he'd escaped from in Bowness was behind him. It was surging after their car and had already engulfed the elderly couple's home.

Charles jammed his foot on the accelerator and blustered the engine to life. The vehicle was bolting along the lake road, with the shadowy water to his left. His speedometer read fifty. Sixty. But the gas quickly overtook the car. It gushed through the vents and into Charles' face.

Charles reached into the back seat. He clutched the couple's dog blanket and dragged it forward, as the toxic fumes billowed into the car. His eyes burning. His throat on fire.

He rammed the dog blanket into Penny's mouth and pinched her nose.

"Don't breathe in, Penny. Don't breathe in!" he spluttered.

Blackened blood sprayed from Charles' nostrils. He felt weak, and the car began to slow down. He started to fade away.

"Don't breathe in. Don't breathe..."

2

Fred gripped the hockey stick and crept towards the basement door. The lock had been busted in, and the door hung on its hinges. He jerked it open and gazed into the blackness below.

Fred flicked on the light switch, and the basement erupted with brightness. He scanned the clutter of boxes that he could glimpse from the top of the stairs. But he couldn't spot the intruder.

"Whoever's down here, you can come out. I've called the police," he called down. But there was no answer.

Fred quietly slid off his slippers and inched down the steps. His foot flesh quietly slapped on the concrete as he went.

He reached the bottom and glanced around the jumbled room in silence.

"Listen, come out," Fred offered. "I don't want to hurt you."

Still nothing. Fred edged deeper into the basement and peeked around every nook and cranny.

Fred spotted an opened tin of baked beans resting on the corner pocket of his snooker table. It was half eaten and had been stabbed through the lid.

He glanced up at the dry food cupboard to his left. It'd been opened, raided, with packets of crisps littering the floor.

Suddenly, Fred heard a shuffling noise behind him. He swung around and held his hockey stick high.

A tall, dark figure emerged from under the stairs. Both its arms were raised, but only one had a hand on the end of it. The other was a gnarled stump where a hand should have been.

"Nice stick, dad," the figure groaned.

Fred lowered the hockey stick. He glimpsed behind the man, and saw a rolled out sleeping bag, a survival backpack and some radios laid out like a nest in the crawlspace under the stairs.

"Ross..." Fred murmured. His poor boy had returned home.

3

James glanced over the steel railing of his second story balcony and decided that the fall wouldn't be enough to end his life. The sand-stone paving tiles below seemed hard enough to do him some damage. Possibly break his spine and turn him into a quadriplegic. Or give him lasting brain damage. He didn't want that for himself. Wouldn't be fair on his son, or his wife. Better to carry on the way things are, for now.

James sucked another smoky kiss from his cigarette and gazed down at the playground in the courtyard below. His son Cassim, a short, chubby five-year-old, was wheezing along with the other children in the football cage. He was under the supervision of the other parents of the apartment building, who were standing at the courtside. James didn't want to be down there with him.

"Father of the year, you are" he whispered to himself.

He heard a dull slamming noise coming from the rooms behind him, and his ears pricked up. The front door. Aisha must be home with the shopping.

James hurriedly tossed the shortened cigarette over the edge. He exhaled the excess smoke and wafted it away with his hands to leave no trace. Aisha perched alongside him at the railing. She was a short woman, with black, bushy hair the way he'd liked. Her scent was lavender and coffee.

"I'll give up smoking, Aisha. I promise," she crowed at him.

"Tough morning," he muttered.

"How was he?"

"Wanted to play out with his friends."

"Jim, you're his dad. He needs you."

"He needs other kids. He's an only child."

"Please."

She touched his hand. The feel of her soft skin against his always made everything better. It was like the good old days, before Cassim. When they were in their early twenties, and free. And before Aisha's affair.

James turned to face her. He gazed into her maple eyes and, for a moment, forgot the cold London skyline around him.

"My mother called," he mumbled.

Aisha gripped the shopping bags at her feet and strode back into the apartment. A sinking feeling returned to James' stomach, and he thought about jumping over the railing's edge again.

James followed her inside the apartment. It smelled like stale bread, and crumbs of old meals gathered on the sides and on the sofa. Aisha was thrusting groceries into their sticky fridge. Pictures of the couple and their son donned the silver cover of it. Happier times, that never really existed in James' heart.

"Don't you want to hear what she has to say?" James queried.

"What did she want?"

"She wants to see Cassim."

Aisha continued her unpacking.

"Aisha", he pressed "it's been twelve months. I don't know what else to do."

"I know you're unhappy here. But this is all Cassim knows now. It's his home."

"I'm not asking to move back. I'm asking to take him to the people that love him. His family."

Aisha returned to loading the fridge.

James stepped forward now, "it's been a tough year for all of us, I know that. That's why mum wants to make amends."

"I swear to God, if you're lying to me again…"

James touched her shoulder. Aisha glanced his hand away and continued, "if we go up and your mum is rude to me, or if your brother is there and you can't control your anger, we're going to have trouble. Our boy doesn't need that."

Aisha marched out of the room. James was left gazing at a photograph on the refrigerator door. It was of Cassim, Aisha and him at a theme park. Happier times.

4

From his position outside at the petrol pumps, James could peer at Aisha clearly through the motorway service station window. She was chatting to some handsome motorcyclist.

James reached into the car at his left and pilfered Aisha's unattended phone. He spun around away from the window and scrolled through her messages.

"Dad, are you playing mum's games?" Cassim howled from the backseat.

"Yes. I'm playing your mum's games."

"Can I play?"

"No."

James reached the bottom of her contacts for that month. Only her co-workers were talking to her, and it seemed strictly about work.

"Here. Play your stupid games," James tossed the phone into the back of the car and turned away from his son. Aisha was paying at the counter and waving her final chirpy goodbyes to the stranger.

"You haven't forgiven her at all, have you? You bastard." James scolded himself under his breath.

5

James shambled out of his car and gazed up at his childhood home. It was a tall, slate farmhouse with a roof that jutted high into the air like an Arthurian tower. He felt the mountain wind stab at his cheeks, as he surveyed the sweeping landscape around it.

Aisha struggled out of the passenger seat and hoisted her son from the rear of the vehicle.

Fred blustered out of the house and strode towards James.

"Jim, boy! How are you?" he boomed. He embraced James tight and whispered into his ear, "we're in danger."

"What?" James hushed.

"I couldn't convince your mother."

Before James could quiz him further, his father darted towards Aisha and hugged her as well.

"Aisha, my lovely! Tell me you've been alright?"

Fred squatted down to meet Cassim, and the boy hid behind his mother's leg.

"And who might this chum be? He's so big."

"Cassim, go on. It's your grandfather," Aisha urged.

Fred opened his arms wide, and Cassim sheepishly entered them for a squeeze.

"Don't worry, lad," Fred reassured him. "It's been strange for me too".

"Fred," a low voice interrupted, and everyone spun around.

Dawn was standing at the doorway of the house and was framed neatly by the stone arch. James noted new frown lines on her face.

Fred grinned at the boy, "See, your Nana's been bursting to see you again."

Dawn bent over slightly and smiled and waved towards Cassim.

"Mum, say hi to Aisha," James asked softly.

Dawn's face snapped back to her signature glower, and she raised her arm towards her grandson.

"Come on, Cassim," she said flatly. "I want to show you to your room."

"No, allow me," Fred grunted. He gripped Aisha and Cassim's arms tight and led them both past Dawn and into the house. "You and Jim obviously need to get reacquainted."

Aisha shot James a final disappointed glance over her shoulder before she disappeared through the archway.

6

The sun had set, and only the faint orange glow of their cigarettes illuminated James and his mother's faces in the darkness. They were squashed together on an old, oak bench in the back garden and were gazing down at the rear of the house.

Through the kitchen window, James could see Aisha in the clear, iridescent light washing a mug at the sink inside.

"Marriage is a tough thing. You're too much like your father," Dawn mumbled.

"You going to keep yapping?" James sniped. "You could have at least said hello to her."

"I feel how I feel. You should know that."

"And you should know it's been a year already. Why don't you want our family back to how it was?"

"Because you've got Cassim."

"You have a problem with my son now?"

"No. You should just concentrate more on raising him safely, than changing my mind. I'll never forgive Aisha for what she did to you."

"She's trying her best and is a good mother. You need to accept that."

Dawn stubbed her cigarette out on the terracotta ashtray to her right. She struggled to her feet, "your son needs stability. I'm sorry you won't find it here".

She hobbled down the slope towards the house. James looked down over the building and to the wide valley beyond. The lake at the foot of the mountain below them glinted in the moonlight. Then James glimpsed something.

Across the night's sky, specks of light were rushing towards Bowness. They were white and red and clustered together in the distance.

Helicopters, James noted.

7

Ivy dabbed the beads of sweat from her forehead and caught her breath. Around her, the doctor's office waiting room was now a flurry of soldiers constructing makeshift beds. Her older colleagues were scrambling to assemble medical apparatus in a frenzy. She was terrified.

Her phone began to buzz. She glanced at the caller ID on the screen. It read James.

She slipped into her office and answered her phone.

"Jim?" she garbled.

"How's my favourite baby sister?"

"Shh. I can't talk now."

"What's wrong? Why are you whispering?"

Ivy opened the door a crack and peered through the gap. The waiting room was now a temporary hospital ward, with soldiers still clambering about.

"The army closed off Bowness this morning," she gulped. "They made us promise not to say anything, but they're using our practice as a trauma centre."

"You serious?"

"Do I sound fucking serious? They have guns with them."

"Are you safe?"

"Look, are you with mum and dad now?"

"We've just arrived."

"Keep your bags packed. I'll be busy with my patients, but I'll call you back with more info when I can. I'm sorry".

Ivy hung up, before James could say goodbye.

8

James descended the staircase and felt the bottom step squeak underfoot. He turned towards the kitchen but stopped.

Through the doorway he could glimpse his parents muttering with a figure. They caught sight of him and immediately ceased conversation. James noticed it was his brother, Ross.

Fred half-inched towards James. "It's ok, son. Don't worry."

"Where's Aisha?" James grunted.

"I sent her outside with Cassim."

James spun around and marched out of the house, and his father dashed out after him.

As he stomped down the sloped driveway towards his car, James felt the bracing night wind against his skin. He spotted Aisha and his son playing together just beside the vehicle. But once they saw him, their happy demeanours dropped.

"Aisha, we're leaving," James barked.

Fred clutched James' arm and yanked him back, and Aisha quickly darted with Cassim towards the back of the house.

James shunted his father off him, "what the hell are you playing at? Bringing him here?", he shouted.

"I didn't bring him here, he showed up."

"And when were you going to tell me?"

James unlocked his car door.

Fred pleaded, "I'm sorry about what happened, but hasn't he suffered enough? He nearly died over there in the army."

"He slept with my wife," James grumbled. "Besides, we have bigger things to deal with right now."

9

Dawn shambled down into the basement and saw Ross fiddling with his soldier's radios. The white noise bleared out from every channel.

"You get back upstairs now," she bleated.

"Fuck off."

"You might not care about your brother, but this rift of yours is killing your dad."

"Mum, I'm trying to see if we're in danger!"

His face looked grave.

"What's happening?" She asked, carefully.

"I thought I just heard a coded transmission. We only use it for emergencies."

"What kind of emergency?"

The white noise on the radio cut out, and was replaced by a slow, electronic beeping. Dawn watched Ross scramble for a pen and scrawl down the cryptic rhythms.

"Something big," Ross murmured.

10

James and his father were still on the driveway. Ross bolted from the house and his mother clambered out behind him.

"Ivy's in trouble!" he bawled, when a huge explosion noise echoed from the horizon, and everyone jerked to see it.

Miles below them, at the east edge of the lake, a colossal fireball was pluming into the sky. Distant gunshots rang out across the valley, as did the faint screams of unseen people.

"Oh my god," Fred muttered.

"That's Bowness down there," James gasped, as he struggled for his phone.

Aisha and Cassim sprinted out from the back of the house and joined the family on the lawn.

Dawn gripped her crucifix necklace. "Ivy," she whispered.

11

Dawn and Fred stood by their flatscreen television. She flipped through channels of static, and Fred fidgeted with an FM radio and tried to get it to work.

At the other end of the living room, Aisha was perched in the wing-backed chair comforting Cassim. She scrambled to get any internet connection on her phone, but with no luck.

"It's weird," Fred huffed. "It's like someone's shut all the signals off."

Ross knelt at the coffee table at the centre, among a mass of bulky, army radios and turned dials to listen intently through an earpiece.

James paced at the large bay-window at the front of the house. He studied the far-off flames below and called Ivy repeatedly on his phone, to no answer.

A call connected –

"Jim?!" Ivy's voice crackled over the phone. All the family clambered to James, as he held the phone high for a better voice-connection.

"Are you ok? What's happening?" James choked.

"We're being attacked! It's –" Gunshots rang out over Ivy's end of the line and obscured her voice.

"Are you hurt?"

"Take the family and get them as far away as you can. I'm sorry!"

"Who's attacking you?" Ross jumped in.

Some static interrupted the line. James heard some indistinct screaming over the call, and then Ivy's voice uttered.

"Dead people".

The connection cut off. Then the lights failed in the house and the family was shrouded in darkness.

12

James had already half-dressed himself in his raincoat by the front door when Aisha tugged on his arm.

"Where the hell are you going?" she hissed.

"You think I'm just going to leave her there to die? She's only forty minutes away."

Fred and Dawn hurtled in from the living room, with Cassim in tow. Ross lingered in the threshold between rooms and surveyed the scene.

"Take that coat off and sit down now," Dawn clamoured.

"Please, think of our boy. He needs you here." Aisha whispered.

Fred dragged Cassim into the back room.

Dawn continued, "you want to be stupid and throw your life away?"

"Ivy's still talking, which is good," he responded. "And there's some soldiers protecting her there, so there's a short window of time where we can bring her here to safety."

"If you ignore the gunshots," Ross interrupted.

"How do you know that?" Dawn asked James. "We don't know anything about what's going on."

"I care about your sister as much as you do," Aisha butted in. "But didn't she tell us to get out of here?"

"That's why Ross will take you and the rest of the family and go," James replied.

"Oh, will I?" Ross chuckled.

"Listen, asshole," James snarled. "I don't like this any more than you."

"And what are you going to do when you get shot at? Talk them to death?"

"Shut up. No one is going anywhere," Dawn commanded.

"If anyone's going to get her, it'll be me," Ross stepped forward. "I'm the only one here with combat experience."

"You're a cripple, and you're unreliable," James said.

"You're a civilian. You've got a kid, you're staying."

"Take your brother, Jim," Aisha quietly cut in. Everyone stared.

She continued, "I've been married to you long enough to know you'll do whatever the hell you want to anyway if it's for your family. At least this time, you'll have a professional looking out for you, to bring you back when it gets too dangerous for you."

"What if she's not at the GP Practise?" Ross queried.

"Then you'll bring him straight back. Promise?"

Ross nodded.

Aisha held James' face, and he gazed down into her maple eyes. They looked petrified.

"Promise?"

13

Ross hoisted the daysack onto his shoulder and thrust a radio into his mother's hands. His parents both looked pale as they congregated with him at the front door.

"I'll need you to keep us updated on what roads to take, in case any get blocked," Ross stated. "I'll check in on the radio every ten minutes. Don't change the frequency."

"I still don't understand why you have to go," Dawn blurted. "It's suicide."

"Suicide's my speciality. And I made a promise to Aisha to keep Jim safe. It'll only be a scouting mission."

Ross slid his combat knife into its holster at his right armpit and peeked outside.

He saw James was hugging Cassim on the driveway, with Aisha nervously biting her lip beside them. They were standing together by Fred's black, four-by-four truck.

Fred clasped Ross's body tight. "Just get home safe," he muttered. "There's no shame in turning around."

Once he let go, Dawn squeezed him a softer, longer embrace.

Ross handed his parents some folded papers. "One more thing. If things get hairy here, you cut and run. Give my boy Smithy a radio on one of these frequencies, and we'll find you."

"Smithy? Your friend?" Fred asked.

"Sergeant now, but he owes me one. Chances are we'll be back in fifteen minutes, without her."

Ross trudged away towards his father's truck.

"This is Aisha's fault." Dawn said. "Her and her big mouth."

14

James and Ross were perched inside their motionless vehicle and scanned the winding road half a mile below them. Through Ross' binoculars, James could see a blockade was forming. Police officers scurried to erect barriers using their cars.

"Looks like we're too late," Ross uttered. "There's no shame in turning back now."

"Then get out and walk home," James replied.

"What are you going to do, genius? There's twenty of them and one of you."

"Ivy doesn't have much time," James barked. "I know her chances are slim, but I want to tell her that we at least tried something."

Ross grabbed the binoculars from him and spied on the path below. "Dad says there's no other way around."

He then pointed down at a field, adjacent to the road. It was shrouded above by a thicket of twisting trees.

"There. Overhead cover."

The brothers turned off their headlights and carefully drove down to the field. Once they were there, they jumped out and silently pushed the car inside. They waited in the ankle-deep dirt.

"What the hell are we waiting for?" James hissed.

"Shh." Ross was surveying the officers through the skeletal branches a hundred meters to their left. It was so quiet, James could hear their individual voices echo over the drizzle.

A fleet of helicopters thundered overhead.

"Sound cover. Go." Ross hushed.

The brothers leapt back into their vehicle. James pressed his foot down on the accelerator, and they skid across the field. They re-joined the asphalt road at the far side and the blue siren lights were now specks on the horizon behind them.

"Suckers," Ross chuckled. "Too slow".

15

James sped along the darkened roadway. The brothers were mute, as raindrops tapped at their windscreen and the engine gently reverberated.

"So, 'dead people'?" Ross queried. "What do you think Ivy meant by that?"

James didn't respond. He'd never believed in such rubbish. He'd hoped Ivy misspoke in the heat of adrenaline.

A figure leaped out in front of the truck. James had no time to turn –

The impact flung both brothers into their seatbelts. James slammed on the brake and the deafening clap of shattered glass punched his eardrums.

The windscreen crackled in front of them, and James glimpsed the figure fly over the roof.

The truck screeched to a halt, and James felt his heart hammering his chest. He unfastened himself and gasped for breath.

Ross clutched his brother's arm, "Where are you going?"

"Out there," James twisted himself free. "They might need help."

"Hang on."

James stumbled out of the vehicle and shambled towards the pitch-black road behind him.

He flicked on his phone's flashlight, then winced at his bruised ribs. On the tarmac surface, a reflective puddle gleamed and trailed off into the shadow behind the truck. But it wasn't blood. This was inky and stunk like chemical bleach.

James followed its oily path and creeped deeper and deeper into darkness.

Then, he saw the body.

He collapsed to his knees. Ross clambered to meet his brother.

The female corpse was a stony grey, with dry, wrinkled skin. Completely hairless and flaky, she seemed almost the size of a teenager. But huge protrusions, like jagged, insect legs jutted from her lifeless body.

"What the fuck?" Ross coughed. "What is she?"

Then, a low, angry cry bellowed out from the shadows.

"Back to the truck. Now." Ross jerked James to his feet.

A terrible, ravenous creature lashed out at them.

The brothers scrambled back into the vehicle and slammed the doors shut, as it was upon them. They fired the engine to life and roared off into the blackness.

The creature just watched as their rear lights faded away. The licence plate read PR13 6FD.

It spun around and carefully regarded the body. It sunk to its knees and wept.

"Penny," It whimpered. "I'm so sorry."

16

Charles advanced on the lone police car and pulled the officer out of the driver's seat. He thrust his claws into the policeman's neck before he could fight back.

Charles hurled the carcass of the officer into a ditch and limped back towards the squad car. He wiped the blood clean from his talons and coughed up a dark grease from his lungs.

All he could think about were the two killers that murdered his daughter and sped off into the night. He knew he was different now – his physique, altered. But he didn't care.

He placed Penny's body on the passenger seat then sat down behind the driver's wheel. He fiddled with the police computer on the dashboard.

He typed in "PR13 6FD".

The computer flashed up a profile on the vehicle – A black pick-up truck, registered to a Fred Bolland. Charles contemplated the address listed. It was just up the mountain. A quick fifteen-minute trip.

Charles twisted the key in the ignition and chambered a round into his nine-millimetre pistol. He was hungry for blood.

17

The deathly stench of gunpowder hung on the air. Shooting and screaming echoed from the distant ravine below.

Both brothers laid with their bellies on the dirt and peered down at Ambleside. The town was a smoking wreck, with several buildings in flames.

Through the binoculars, James could spot soldiers clad in gasmasks. They were scurrying through the warrens between smoky, stone buildings. Some were kicking open doors and firing their weapons. Some had civilians with them.

In another street, James saw a lone soldier blasting his sidearm at a crowd of people who were charging at him. Once they reached him, they sunk their teeth into his body and jumped on him.

James thrusted the binoculars back into Ross' hand. "It can't be like this everywhere?" He trembled.

"Everywhere between us and Ivy. Radio chatter's full of it."

"What do we do?"

"Head home."

"But Ivy?"

Ross grasped James' collar and shook him. "Listen here, you moron. I made a promise to your wife to bring you back, and I'm keeping it. We tried our best, but we have to leave. Now."

Ross struggled up and pushed his way through the bushes towards the truck.

"Fuck," James gulped. He got up and followed.

18

James shinnied down the steep rock path after his brother. The spiked overgrowth around him scraped at his raincoat as he descended towards the road.

Ahead, Ross was barking into his walkie-talkie. "Smithy, it's Bolland. Come in. Over."

"What are you doing?" James asked.

"My old squad will be out there fighting. If we can't get to Ivy, maybe they can."

Ross uttered back into his radio. "Smithy, if you can hear this, I'm stuck at Acorn Medical Practice in Troutbeck Bridge. There're civilians with me. Mostly doctors. We need an evac. Over."

A cold silence echoed in response from the radio. Ross repeated his call again and again as they crept their way down the embankment.

James and Ross stumbled out of the shrubbery and found themselves back at the roadside.

A dark figure was inspecting their father's battered truck, so Ross ripped out his knife and advanced on him.

"Back the fuck up!" Ross demanded. He pointed the serrated edge at the stranger, who leapt backwards with his hands up.

"Calm down, see? I'm not bitten. I'm clean," the figure yelped. He was a soldier in his forties and had no weapon on him.

"Ross, look at his uniform," James pleaded.

"What are you doing here?" Ross growled at the man.

"I was checking to see if there were any survivors in this van. My name's Hyland. Corporal Steve Hyland."

"Where's your weapon?"

"Sir, those things will be here any minute."

James pushed Ross' outstretched arm down, lowering the knife. Hyland dropped his hands too.

"What's going on?" James queried.

"You were saying Acorn Med Centre on your radio before?" Hyland gestured. "That's where my boys are held up. We took a pounding, but we're ok."

"Are there doctors there?"

"A few. You looking for someone?"

"Our sister," James blurted. "Dr Ivy Bolland –"

"But we're on our way home," Ross interrupted.

"Not that way, you're not," Hyland signalled behind him. "The fields are crawling with them now. They sent me out this way to recon ahead, but I barely made it back. Those freaks ripped my gear off."

"What the hell are they?" Ross questioned.

"Fuck if I know. But if you get bitten – That's how it spreads. It's a disease."

Suddenly, a ghastly cry cut through the night air.

"Listen," Hyland gasped. "You let me in your truck, and I'll take you to your sister. It's safe, but we have to go now."

The brothers shared a glance. Then James motioned to the vehicle, and Hyland rushed into the rear seat. The brothers hoisted themselves in too, and the three men screeched off into the distance.

"Acorn Med Centre, Troutbeck Bridge," Hyland caught his breath. "It's just five clicks away."

Hyland had his hand on the button of his two-way radio. He was secretly broadcasting their conversation.

19

A panicked thumping rattled the hinges of the closed front door. "Let me in! Please!" a voice hollered from outside.

Fred clutched onto his hockey stick and peeked out of the window. Aisha gripped Cassim close to her body and watched with Dawn from the hallway.

"It's a woman," Fred said.

He heaved the door open, and a platinum blonde lady flung herself inside. She was wearing a business suit, but it was covered in dirt.

Fred slammed the door behind her. He moved to comfort the gasping stranger, but she jolted at his touch. Dawn rushed to help him.

The couple lugged the woman off into the kitchen, and Aisha stroked Cassim's hair.

"Don't worry, Cas," she calmed herself. "Everything's going to be alright".

20

The woman shivered and wrapped herself in a blanket at the far end of the kitchen. "My name's Gail," she muttered.

The family perched around her in the candlelight. Fred was still holding his hockey stick. Cassim was away from the adults in the adjoining room.

"We need to leave here," Gail jabbered. "It's not safe."

"What do you mean?" Fred questioned.

"What do you think I mean? Those things are on their way!"

"Those creatures Ross radioed about before," Aisha carefully said to Fred.

"You all think I'm crazy," Gail continued.

"We don't," Fred cut her off. "We're just trying to understand. Our family is out there."

"Look, I only just made it here from Rydal on foot," Gail said. "It doesn't matter if you're tucked away up here. Sooner or later, they'll find us and kill us all."

Aisha shared a fearful glance with her in-laws.

"Dawn, love?" Fred asked. "Pack the car and bring some provisions. Aisha, help Gail clean herself up."

"But what about our boys?" Dawn interrupted.

"We're not going just yet. We made a promise to stay and help them. But better safe than sorry."

Dawn left the room. Aisha put a hand on Gail's shoulder.

"Come on," she smiled. "You've been through a lot. You're safe now."

But Aisha didn't believe it.

21

The brothers opened the heavy door of the doctor's office waiting room and Ross flashed his torchlight inside. Bodies littered the floor, as did the mangled detritus of steel cots.

"Hyland, perimeter check. Over." Ross breathed into his radio.

"No visual. All clear, outside. What happened to my boys in there? Over."

Ross kicked the nearest corpse. It didn't move.

"Check these doctors," he mumbled to James.

He slid further into the blackness and began searching the adjoining offices.

James trembled, as he crouched over the first body. The walls around him were pockmarked with bullet holes and splashes of wet claret.

The deep gashes on the body made the doctor unrecognisable. These people were ripped apart by something. He rummaged for the ID badge. It wasn't Ivy – a relief.

James waded through the rest of the room and scanned for as many badges as he could. A sickly stench of iron invaded his nostrils.

James finished checking all the doctors, then huddled himself into Ivy's office and squatted down in the corner with his back against the wall. He felt the tears build up in his face, so he clenched his eyelids shut in the darkness.

Ross barged in, "we've got to go."

"Ivy's not here."

"Then she's smarter than we are."

"All the doctors are accounted for. She got away."

"This place was attacked by God knows what, and we don't even have a weapon to defend ourselves."

"Weapons," James said. He jolted to his feet, elbowed past Ross, and moved back into the main waiting room.

James sifted through the bodies again, this time focussing on the soldiers. "Give me your light," he huffed.

Ross beamed his brother with the torch.

"None of these soldiers have their guns," James turned. "Isn't that weird?"

Ross' face dropped. He called over his radio to Hyland. There was no response. He rushed to the window and glanced outside.

"Fuck. Hyland's gone," Ross muttered.

A gunshot splintered the glass by Ross' head. A typhoon of bullets shredded the windows around them and both brothers dived on the floor for cover.

Ross clambered through the raining shards and hauled James up by his collar. He yanked his brother towards the fire escape at the rear of the building.

"Smithy, we're under attack. Come in!" Ross bawled over the radio. The gun-claps muffled his voice.

They were about to pile out of the exit, when James stopped him. He pointed through the door's window.

Outside, a group of figures were shambling from the treeline towards them. They were holding army rifles and had rotten, insect legs poking out of their backs.

The figure at the head of the pack hoisted his gun up at them. James and Ross leapt to their right, as more bullets pounded through the concrete. Dust flew into their mouths, as the brothers scrambled to reach Ivy's office to safety.

They jammed the door shut, and Ross heaved the filing cabinets in front to block it.

"Get under there," Ross signalled to Ivy's desk. James scuffled underneath.

Ross rammed his back against the wall and slid down to his heels. "Smithy," he spluttered into his radio, "For fuck's sake, we're surrounded. Twelve plus foot-mobiles closing in on our position. We're unarmed. Over."

A huge boom rattled the building. Foam ceiling tiles plummeted down on the brothers.

"Copy, Bolland," a gruff voice crackled over the line. "Stay put, while we advance on your position. ETA one minute."

"Took your time! We're on the south side of the building. First floor, rear office. Watch your fire."

"What do we do?" James shrieked.

Ross unsheathed his knife and locked his eyes on the door. "Pray," he grimaced.

More explosion sounds erupted from outside, and the gunfire noises doubled.

Ross' radio blustered again, "Bolland, make your way down the main staircase. Now."

"Copy," Ross shouted.

He darted to James and scooped him out from under the table.

The brothers hefted the cabinets from the door. Ross forced James' head low and stormed into the waiting room with him.

Two soldiers kicked-in the door ahead of them and thrust their barrels into James' face.

Ross raised his hand and dropped the knife.

One soldier forced the brothers down onto their fronts, while the other scanned the room. James peeked up and saw that they both had gasmasks on.

The soldier above them frisked their necks and wrists.

"No bites!" he confirmed to his partner.

He hoisted the siblings to their feet and called to his comrade to regroup.

"Just you two?" the soldier signalled to the brothers.

Ross nodded.

They led the brothers back down the stairs and to outside. The gunshots were so loud that James thought his ears were bleeding.

As they sprinted across the grass towards two armoured vehicles, James glanced behind him.

Soldiers had taken up tactical firing positions around the husk of the doctor's office building and formed a perimeter. They were blasting up at the attackers, who'd been pushed all the way back to the treeline.

The soldiers threw smoke grenades to cover their escape and headed back to the vehicles.

James spotted one soldier being hauled away into the fumes by two creatures.

A trooper pushed James' head down into the dark vehicle and locked the door behind him.

***

Charles clutched his rifle and wafted the smoke away with his hands. His friends were retreating all around him back into the forest.

He coughed and spluttered as the fog cleared. The army vehicles were gone. So were the brothers.

22

The brothers were squashed in the back of the speeding troop-transport vehicle amongst Smithy's squad. They jostled as the truck bounced over bumps. James felt nauseous.

A soldier crammed a cold thermometer into James' ear. He removed it then gave a thumbs up to the rest of the men.

Smithy was sitting on the bench opposite James. "Status?" he asked.

"Hannon's gone," a voice cried. "They fucking dragged him off while we exfilled."

"These bastards don't take prisoners," Smithy responded. "We all know the rules. He's gone."

"Smithy, I'm so sorry –" Ross muttered.

"We volunteered for this," Smithy interrupted. "You're our brother."

"Thank you for saving us," James trembled.

"Apologies for the radio silence. We had reports that the infected were taking army supplies. Couldn't guarantee they weren't eavesdropping."

"How could they attack us like that?" Ross queried. "The ones we've seen up until now were just rabid?"

"The infection destroys your brain and drops your body temperature. You're one of them within hours. But some infected keep their intelligence. We don't know what they want."

"Why is all this happening?" James asked.

"Above our paygrade. We're just here to evac civilians."

"Our sister is still out there. You can help us."

"Negative. If she's not with us now, she's gone."

"How can you say that? You just said you're here to save people?"

"Everyone at that doctor's office was dead. The only reason this mission got priority was because Bolland radioed that there were medical personnel still alive there."

"You can't just let people die."

"Everyone needs our help. We lost a good man saving you."

"Our family is trapped in a house north of here," Ross cut in. "Near Grasmere."

"I'll call it in to the top brass. But that's all I can do."

"My wife and child are there." James asserted. "Are they above your paygrade too?"

"We all have families. You're lucky you're getting evacuated at all."

The driver of the vehicle shouted into his radio "Echo Squad approaching the hotel. ETA 3 minutes."

"You saved my life once before" Smithy said to Ross. "Now, I call us even".

23

Aisha, Fred, Dawn and Gail were perched on the front lawn. They gazed down at the winding mountain road below them, as sirens and gunshots echoed.

"See!" Gail cried. "I told you they'd be coming!"

Fred watched through his binoculars. "The police blockade the boys found. It's broken," he muttered.

He passed the binoculars to Aisha. Through them, she glimpsed the blue flashing lights a mile down the path. Silhouettes of figures were scrambling over the vehicles.

"We head to mum's house, then," Dawn grunted. "Now."

Fred led the women back into the house. Dawn grabbed Cassim and rushed him back outside to the car. Aisha and Gail hastily ferried the remaining boxes of supplies from the kitchen to the vehicle.

Police cars whizzed past the house and fled into the mountains, as the family finished loading their trunk.

Aisha caught sight of some figures sprinting up the roadway towards them.

"Get inside! Now!" Fred brandished his hockey stick.

Aisha dashed into the rear of the vehicle next to Cassim and Gail. Dawn flung herself into the driver's seat.

One of the figures bolted towards Fred, and he cracked the creatures' skull with his weapon. Blood splattered Aisha's window and it tumbled into the dirt. Aisha shielded Cassim's eyes.

Fred climbed into the car, and the family sped away up the road to follow the police.

"You alright?" Dawn asked her husband.

"Keep driving, dear."

Aisha glanced through the rear window of the car. More monsters were piling into their house and chasing after them. They were getting smaller in the distance.

Fred clutched the walkie-talkie. "James, Ross. Come in. We're ok, but the house has been overrun. Don't go back there. We're on our way to Nan's. Over."

24

Two soldiers shoved James out of the Humvee and onto the cobbled driveway. He gazed up at the Victorian hotel to his right. The sign read "The Ingledene Inn".

A sniper was posted on the roof, and soldiers scurried around the chain-link fence at the building's perimeter.

Smithy's squad led James and Ross up the stone staircase to the main entrance. Inside, the foyer was a wide room with a large chandelier.

"Welcome to sanctuary, lads," Smithy said. "Phillips and Gomez will take care of you until the next evac convoy arrives."

"Please," James begged. "Let us go. Our family's still out there."

Smithy ignored him and exited the hotel. He jumped back into his Humvee with some troopers and sped out of the hotel grounds.

Two soldiers grabbed the brothers from behind and pulled them away. James thrashed against them.

James then glimpsed a woman being dragged into the main entrance by a squad. She had dark hair and a white medical coat on. It was Madeline Hague, a doctor from Ivy's office.

"My daughter," she cried. "You have to find her!"

25

With his hands up, Hyland approached the front gate of the hotel. The guards pointed their rifles at him and yelled, so he got down onto his front.

They searched him for bites and hastily checked his temperature. Then, they dragged him inside.

A trooper behind the gate searched his bag. "Where the hell did you come from, Corporal?"

"Bowness," Hyland muttered. "My platoon got jumped, but I got away with this ordinance."

"Fuck me." The soldier lifted out some C4 explosive charges from the bag.

"I heard over the radio you were evacuating some civilians from here," Hyland continued. "I figured you could use an assist."

"Where's the rest of your squad?"

Hyland shook his head.

The guard returned Hyland's bag to him and signalled towards the main hotel building. "Head on up. Gomez will want to see this. He's in charge."

Hyland moved towards the hotel. He entered the main foyer and a blonde, female private saluted him.

"You're here for Sergeant Gomez, sir?" she asked.

Hyland nodded.

"He's on the first floor. Room eleven."

"Thank you, Private," Hyland replied.

He climbed the grand staircase. There was less activity on the upper floors, so he made it all the way to the roof.

He exited onto the walkway at the top of the building to find the sniper crouched at the battlements with his gun pointing down at the horizon.

"You lost, sir?" he asked Hyland without looking away from his scope.

There was a pile of bricks to Hyland's left. He reached for one and cracked the soldier across the back of his skull. The sniper fell unconscious and Hyland grabbed his rifle.

"Roof clear," Hyland whispered into his radio.

He pulled out the C4 from the bag and planted it behind the air vents.

"Charges set," he radioed.

Hyland dashed to the fire escape and climbed down off the roof.

26

James was sitting across from Madeline at the hotel restaurant table. She was shivering.

At the end of the room, Ross was pleading with two armed soldiers who were guarding the exit towards the main foyer.

The dining area around James was mostly empty, except for a few survivors huddled together around camping lights.

Ross sat back down at the table. "Well, that was useless," he grunted. "They're keeping us here for a while."

"Are you alright, Maddie?" James asked. "Where's your daughter?"

"Jim, just give her a minute," Ross interrupted.

James passed Madeline his water bottle, and she drank.

"...What the hell are you two idiots doing here anyway?" She muttered. "I thought you were still down in London?"

"We were at the medical centre looking for Ivy," James replied. "Were you there tonight?"

"It was a fucking mess... Our own patients attacked us. Ivy got away."

"Where is she?"

"I don't know. We got split up... She has my daughter."

"Your daughter was with you there?" Ross cut in.

"I thought we'd be safe together with the soldiers protecting us," Madeline responded. "It's my own stupid fault..."

James held her hand, "Maddie, please. I know we haven't always been friends. But if there's any information you can tell us..."

"...Belle Isle. I think the soldiers wanted to move us there before the attack."

"What's Belle Isle?"

"It's a private hospital out on the lake island. We tried to evacuate to it, but..." Madeline covered her eyes to hide her tears. "I hope to Christ they got there," she mumbled.

"Soldiers of the Ingledene Inn," a monstrous voice boomed over the guards' radios. Everyone turned.

"Your colleague Private Hannon is with me," it said.

"Please! Don't kill me –" Another voice cried in the background.

"What the fuck?" James whispered.

"There are two brothers in your custody," the voice asserted again. "James and Ross Bolland. Release them to me, and Hannon lives. If not, everyone in that hotel will die. You have three minutes."

People in the dining area jumped up and ran for the door. One of the guards quickly grabbed his comrade's radio, dashed out of the exit, and closed it behind him to block them.

"We need to leave," Ross murmured. "Now."

27

James barged his way through the small crowd towards the door guard.

"My friend's not breathing!" James exclaimed. "Please, you have to help. He's in the bathroom!"

The soldier locked the exit and pushed his way through the people with James. "Everyone, sit back down," he bellowed. "The situation is under control."

James and the soldier walked down the long, winding hallway to the restrooms. "He's in there," James pointed at the men's room door.

The soldier stepped inside. Ross leapt out from behind him.

The trooper spun around, and Ross gripped the man's rifle. They wrestled against the tight walls.

The soldier reached for his knife. Ross clutched the man's arm to stop him. He pushed the soldier down hard onto the ground tiles.

He didn't move. Ross checked his breathing.

James crept inside. "Holy shit," he whispered.

"How are we looking out there?" Ross muttered.

"Grab his key."

Ross snatched the soldier's gun then took the keys.

"Fuck. No radio," Ross said.

The brothers exited the bathroom. Ross pointed the gun at the few survivors and directed them away from the door.

"We are leaving." He quietly stated. "You're all free to do the same. No one tell the guards, or there'll be trouble."

James unlocked the door behind the bar which led towards outside.

"Jim, what the fuck?!" Madeline asked.

"Ivy's at Belle Isle," he replied. "That's where we're headed."

"But it's suicide!"

"We can't stay. You people will be killed if we do. I'm sorry."

"And what if they attack us anyway?"

"Help us find where this place is," James insisted. "We're going to save your daughter."

28

Charles was hidden amongst the overgrowth on the cliffside across the road. He scanned the hotel far below him.

His friends were loading their weapons. He had a radio in one hand and a detonator in the other. Private Hannon was bloodied and tied up in the dirt.

"This is Sergeant Gomez," the radio blustered. "Identify yourself. Over."

"Do you have what I want?" Charles replied.

"Negative. These people are under our protection. Any attempt on our compound will be met with deadly force. You have been warned. Over."

Charles waited. Then he clicked the detonator.

The hotel erupted into a ball of flame. The deafening blast hurled bricks into the air. The shockwave hit Charles' comrades and knocked them back.

The building below was a smoking wreck. Soldiers writhed on the ground outside.

Charles stood up and cocked his rifle.

"Let's go."

29

James, Ross and Madeline sprinted down the wooden steps towards the docks. Some survivors followed, then trailed off into the woodland by themselves.

James glanced back up at the blazing hotel on the cliffside behind him. Screaming and gunfire echoed.

"Keep moving!" Ross shouted.

The brothers scrambled down the pier towards the motorboats. James and Madeline unmoored one. Ross smacked the lock off the boathouse door with his rifle.

Ross entered and grabbed the boat's ignition key, before darting back outside.

"Drop the gun!" a harsh voice hollered.

James looked up –

Hyland had a rifle pointing into Ross' back. Ross had his arms up. Hyland took his gun from him and tossed it into the lake.

"Hyland? Why?" James gasped.

"Shut up and get on the floor."

James and Madeline lay down on their fronts. Ross knelt.

Hyland called into his radio, "Charles, I have the two brothers on the pier. Over."

"Hyland, please," James muttered. "Our sister –"

"I said shut it," Hyland replied. "You two are killers. You're both going to pay for what you did."

"And what the hell was that?" Ross asked.

Hyland whacked Ross with his rifle-butt.

Another explosion blasted from the hotel. It shook the docks, and fragments rained down. Hyland flinched, and Ross leapt up and grabbed him.

The two men tussled. James dashed towards them –

"No!" Ross called back to him. "Take Maddie and go!"

James bolted into the boathouse and grabbed another key. He pushed Madeline into a boat.

Ross reached for Hyland's gun. Hyland swept his feet and landed on top of him. Ross grasped Hyland's collar and yanked him close – pinning the weapon between them both.

Hyland thrusted his knife towards Ross, but he intercepted it. He clasped Hyland's forearm with his right hand.

Hyland's knife inched closer to Ross' neck.

James saw this. He grabbed a boat's oar and scrambled to help his brother.

James pelted Hyland across the face with the heavy wood. Hyland fell. Ross clambered to his feet –

Hyland's body lay lifelessly on the walkway. His skull was split, and blood poured from his brain into the water.

"Fuck…" Ross caught his breath.

Ross took Hyland's radio, rifle and knife.

Another explosion boomed from the hotel. Ross grabbed his brother and hauled him back to the boat.

They dashed into the boat and rocketed off with Madeline across the lake.

30

Charles stood over Hyland's corpse. His infected friends frantically searched the docks around him.

"A boat's missing," one of them yelled. "They must have gone across the lake."

"Hyland..." Charles muttered.

He knelt and carefully took Hyland's dog tags. Then he glanced up at the still, black lake.

"Take a boat and follow," he ordered. "I know where those bastards are going."

31

The boat thundered across the lake. James sat behind the wheel, with Madeline next to him. Ice wind and specks of freezing water battered their faces.

Ross reloaded Hyland's rifle at the other end of the boat.

"Echo Squad to Command," the radio called. "We've taken heavy casualties at the hotel. Over."

"That's Hannon's voice," Ross asserted.

James cut the engine off.

"Copy that, Echo Squad," Command responded. "What's your sit-rep? Over."

"They're all dead. It's just me left... The brothers, they... Killed everyone."

"Command this is Echo Two Three," Ross tried to interrupt. "Come in."

He clicked the button on the radio but got no response. "Fuck. The output's damaged," he grunted.

Ross opened the back panel and fiddled with the wires.

Hannon's voice continued, "...two evacuees, Ross and James Bolland. They are armed and extremely hostile. They set off an explosive device inside the perimeter-"

"Hannon's being forced to say this," James interjected. "To stop us from relying on the army again for help."

"If they believe this crap, we'll be next on the top brass's shit-list," Ross remarked.

"You killed that man," Madeline said.

"Hyland tried to hurt us," Ross replied. "He led us into a trap at the med centre before."

"If you two hadn't have been at the hotel, none of those people would have died."

"She's right," James stated. "Whoever Hyland's been working for – this Charles… They've been after us from the start."

James reignited the boat's engine. "We killed those people at the hotel as soon as we stepped through the door."

32

Aisha and Fred stood at the dining table in Nan's old kitchen. Neil, a neighbour, was with them holding a box of food.

At the other end of the room, Cassim was playing with some wooden toys. Gail was slumped in the dusty armchair with her head in her hands.

"Dawn said you had to make a quick getaway from home," Neil muttered. He put the box on the table. "We thought you lot could do with some supplies."

"Thanks," Fred smiled. "Is it just us that's left in this village?"

"Most people ran when they heard what was going on. But this is my home. And Nan was a good neighbour to me when she was alive."

"How many people have passed through here since?" Aisha queried.

"Relax," Neil said. "We're miles away from anyone here. You're safe."

Fred hugged Neil. Then Neil left.

"...Don't worry," Fred reassured Aisha. "James will radio soon."

Dawn stepped out from the back room, holding a long, double-barrelled shotgun. She snapped the lever into place.

"Someone keep a lookout," she demanded.

33

James, Ross and Madeline sat silently in the stationary boat as it bobbed on the waves. They scanned the lake island two hundred metres away.

James tried to squint through the cold drizzle. The island was dark and eerily still. All he could glimpse was the ornate dome of the hospital poking out of the treetops.

"We can't see shit from here," Ross mumbled. "Get us closer."

James drove to the shoreline. Once there, Ross leapt out of the boat with the rifle. He waded his way up towards the trees.

"Wait here," he said. "I'm scouting ahead."

"Like hell you're going alone," James replied. He jumped out of the boat too.

"James, stay with Maddie –"

"I've already got my hands dirty saving your life once".

James turned to Madeline. "Stay here and guard the boat," he said. "If anything happens, you drive away. If we're not back in ten minutes leave us."

She nodded. She watched the brothers disappear into the forest. But, once she was sure they were gone, she turned the key in the ignition and raced away.

34

James and Ross crept through the trees towards the hospital. It was a tall, repurposed stately home. They halted at the forest's edge and scanned down at the driveway. A few bodies were strewn on the asphalt. Apart from the rain, it was silent.

"Something's not right," Ross mumbled.

"Let's check inside," James said. "Quick."

The brothers followed the treeline towards the side of the building. They found a broken window and climbed in.

They landed in a dark, wood-panelled office. Papers and glass shards littered the floor. Ross quietly led James out into the hallway with his rifle up.

The siblings inched down the shadowy corridor. They rounded a bend and spotted a festering corpse.

James gagged at the stench. Ross squatted to inspect it. It was a soldier in yellow hazmat gear. His guts were ripped, and flies circled.

"He's a day old at least," Ross grimaced. He took the Glock pistol from the body.

James pointed to a pair of half-opened steel shutters at the end of the hall.

The brothers edged towards them. Inside, they glimpsed a tiled chamber with more corpses. Some were wearing white coats.

"Christ," James whispered. "You think she's in here?"

Ross handed James a gasmask from a row of hooks on the wall. He took one for himself, and they both put them on.

They forced the shutters open and squeezed into the chamber. James inspected the badge on one of the doctors. "...They're scientists," he said.

They walked through the plastic curtains into the next room.

It was a wide, long, and windowless laboratory. Rows of desks with apparatus filled the centre. Dimly lit glass cubicles made up the walls. Some had reptiles and insects inside. Others were smashed.

"We should leave," Ross grunted. "Now."

"No. If she's in here, we need to know."

The brothers descended the iron staircase.

James glimpsed at a lit monitor on a desk. A video of a scientist was playing silently. James turned up the volume. It said, "... the failed animal testing results of airborne virus RVNT –"

James opened some crumpled notes on the table and read them.

The video continued, "while all test subjects gain impressive strength and the ability to regrow lost limbs, they're also affected by varied states of psychosis and horrific mutations –"

"... They were trying to heal amputee soldiers with this shit," James said.

Ross glimpsed at some waist-high gas canisters stacked in the corner. Each had a biohazard symbol on it.

"Subjects exposed to the gas," the video went on, "labelled 'Infected Type A', spread the virus through saliva and bodily fluids, but return to a normal cognitive state in a few hours. However, those bitten, labelled 'Infected Type B', remain hyperaggressive and act on instinct –"

A roar cried out. Ross spun and aimed his gun.

A glass cubicle was illuminated at the end of a hallway. A gang of infected people were crammed inside. They thrashed but were trapped behind the blooded glass.

"...They tried to contain an outbreak here," James muttered.

A massive explosion from outside shook the lab. The brothers stumbled, as the metal ceiling gantry crashed down from above.

The glass containing the infected was cracking.

"Come on!" Ross cried. He hauled James back towards the stairs.

James grabbed some laminated papers from the desk and stuffed them into his raincoat pocket.

The cubicle window behind them shattered open and the infected poured out. They scrambled over each other in a blood-soaked frenzy.

James and Ross dashed back out through the lab's main shutter doors. They tried to force them closed.

Snarling erupted from the hallway behind them. They turned and saw that the dead bodies they'd passed on the driveway were now sprinting towards them.

Ross blasted them with his rifle. The gunfire pounded James' eardrums. The charging infected staggered but continued to race forward.

Ross kicked in a door to their left.

Another fireball from outside shuddered the building. The glass windows in the hallway burst open, as the brothers dived through the doorway. They slammed it closed behind them.

Angry thumping battered the other side of the door. The brothers were trapped in a narrow, dark stairway that led up. James felt tiny flecks of glass pricking into his skin.

"Let's move," Ross shouted. He thrust the Glock pistol into James' hands. Together they struggled up the staircase.

As the brothers clambered onto the third story landing, a jet engine roared overhead. James glanced out of the window.

Two harrier jump-jets swooped over the building. More explosions blasted the ground.

"The flyboys are trying to bury this place," Ross clamoured. "With us in it!"

35

Neil blustered through Nan's front door. Fred, Dawn, Aisha, Cassim, and Gail spun around.

"Come quick!" He cried. "My wife, she's stopped moving!"

"What happened?" Fred asked.

"There's no time. Please!"

Fred handed the shotgun to Dawn. "Keep everyone safe here," he ordered.

"And what about you?" Dawn said.

"I'll be back soon."

"Do you need any help?" Aisha cut in.

"Stay put. I'll radio if there's any trouble."

Fred scooped up his hockey stick. He exited the house with Neil.

Unseen by the rest of the family, Gail snuck out of the rear exit of the cottage and into the night.

36

Fred sprinted along the abandoned cobbled street. Freezing rain pummelled his skin.

Neil rushed further ahead. "This way! Quick!" He bawled.

"Hang on!" Fred called back.

Neil disappeared around the back of a cottage. Fred struggled to catch up. He rounded the corner.

Fred saw a gang of creatures waiting in the shadows for him. They raised their rifles.

The last thing Fred thought about were his two sons. The monsters shot him dead.

37

Aisha and Dawn heard the gunshots ring out across the village. Dawn gripped the shotgun. She darted to the kitchen window.

Bullets from outside shattered the glass. Dawn dived onto the ground. Aisha shielded Cassim with her body.

Dawn blasted the shotgun out of the window.

"Get up!" She cried to Aisha. She dragged Aisha and Cassim into the back room.

Dawn flung the basement door open.

"Down there. Now." She bellowed.

"Where's Gail?" Aisha replied.

"Just fucking do as I say! Use the coal chute to climb up into the next street. Get Cassim somewhere safe."

"What about you and Fred?"

Gunfire from outside pounded through the wall. Wood splintered everywhere.

"I said go!" Dawn shoved Aisha and Cassim down into the cellar. She slammed the door and reloaded.

38

James and Ross sprinted around a corner as explosions shook the hospital and debris rained down all around. The doorway ahead of them burst open and a rabble of infected swarmed out. The brothers spun around to flee, but the hallway behind them began to collapse into the building below.

Ross hauled James into a storeroom. He slammed the door behind him and barred it shut with a metal shelving unit. The room rattled. The infected punched through the wood of the door and reached in.

James spotted a large vent at the base of a wall. He kicked in the grate and crawled inside. "This way!" he shouted.

Ross followed him, just as the door ruptured open behind him. The brothers squeezed through the narrow vents. They glanced back to see that the infected behind them had squashed in at the same time and gotten stuck.

James and Ross scurried around each bend.

"The fuck are we going?!" Ross asked.

James entered a junction in the shaft and turned left. A bloodied scientist with yellow infected eyes and no legs scrambled towards him. James blasted a bullet through the creature's skull.

"You ok?" Ross yelled.

James tried to calm himself and moved forward.

The brothers reached a vent that sloped down several floors to the outside. They slid down it, crashed out of the grate at the other side and landed in an alleyway.

James yanked his gasmask off. He could breathe again. Another jet roared overhead. James scooped his brother up and limped towards the shoreline. Once they reached the lake, an explosion twenty metres away blasted soil into the sky. The shockwave hit the brothers and flung them hard into the ice-cold water.

39

Cassim tugged on Aisha as she hoisted herself out of the coal chute's exit in the sodden alleyway.

"What about Grandma?" Cassim asked.

"Shh. Don't worry, sweetie. It'll be alright."

She picked Cassim up and peered over the head-height wall. In the next street, infected figures scurried about. They held guns and dragged Dawn's corpse out of Nan's house.

"Don't look," Aisha whispered. She shielded Cassim's eyes.

The creatures dumped Dawn's body on the street next to Fred's. Gail stood next to the mutant in charge and shouted orders.

"There was a woman and her kid in there too. Find them!"

The other infected spread out into the village. Neil was held back by two of the creatures.

"You bastard!" he called. "You said you'd let my wife go if I helped you! I got one of them out of the house, didn't I?"

The infected dragged him off into a side street.

Aisha crept to the end of the alley with Cassim. "It's ok," she muttered. "Mummy's getting you out of here."

Mutants searched the main road. Once their backs were turned, she darted out into the street with her son and disappeared into the opposite alleyway.

She followed the dark passage until she reached the edge of the village. Aisha put Cassim down and they ran up the country lane. Once they were over the hill, they spotted an abandoned police car.

"We can use this!" Cassim blurted.

Aisha noticed that the front seats were smeared with blood and a dark, viscous liquid. "I don't think so," she said.

"Help! Please!" A muffled voice cried.

Cassim pointed at the vehicle's boot. "Someone's in there!"

Thumping banged from the inside, so Aisha yanked Cassim away.

"Don't leave me!" The voice yelped again. "Please. The monsters will come back!"

It sounded like a child's voice. Aisha didn't know what to do. They couldn't open the car without the key. If they touched it, the alarm might go off.

Aisha scooped up a rock. She smashed the rear passenger window and the vehicle's alarm screeched. She flung the door open, folded down the back seat and saw that a small, terrified girl was crammed inside the boot. Aisha hoisted her out. She clutched Cassim's hand and sprinted with the children towards the forest.

40

James swam with Ross in the freezing water towards the mainland. Ross' head was bleeding, so James pulled his delirious brother the last twenty yards to shore.

"Stay with me," James mumbled. "We're almost there."

More explosions erupted from Belle Isle and debris splashed down all around them. They crawled onto dry land and James checked Ross' headwound.

"... Get the fuck off me..." Ross grumbled.

James glanced back at the flaming hospital on the horizon. Then he spotted a boat full of infected armed with rifles speeding towards them from the north side of the lake.

"Come on!" James shouted. He hoisted his brother up. They dashed into the treeline together.

As the brothers struggled up the hill, they passed the torn corpse of a soldier in the dirt. James took the body's radio and sidearm, then dragged Ross further up the incline. They reached a cave and dived inside. A pale-looking Ross dropped to his knees and held his bleeding head, whilst James shivered. The night wind numbed their soaking bodies.

James tuned the radio to his family's frequency. "Aisha," he said into it. "It's me. Come in."

"Your wife's not here now," a low voice replied.

"Who the hell is this?"

"You know who this is. I found your family. They're dead."

"... It's Charles," Ross muttered.

"Bullshit," James grunted back into the radio.

"I'm at Nan's house where they were hiding," the voice responded. "Your parents' bodies are at my feet. I'm on their radio."

James' legs felt weak. He sat down on a rock.

"You should have just let us kill you at the doctor's office," the voice continued. "Cassim would still be alive."

"I'm going to fucking kill you."

"Like you did Hyland? I'm heading to Bowness. Your sister's there. I'm going to finish the job."

"You don't know where she is."

"Take that risk. See how many more people you can lose. I'll be there."

James sat motionless as tears rolled down his face.

"He's bluffing..." Ross mumbled. "Aisha and Cassim are fine."

James wiped his eyes. He stood and clenched his sidearm. "Get up," he said.

41

Clutching the small girl in her arms, Aisha sprinted with Cassim through the forest. She glimpsed a crashed army jeep that was smashed against a boulder, so she put the girl down and turned to Cassim.

"Mummy's going to check this out," she said. "I need you to be strong and take care of the girl. If I shout, you run."

Cassim nodded.

Aisha approached the wrecked vehicle. Inside, there was some blood, but no sign of the soldiers. She found a torn map and a radio jammed in the footwell, so she took them, then gestured for the kids to come over.

She remembered that Ross said his army friends might be able to help them if there was trouble, so she changed the radio's frequency. "Hello, Smithy?" she called into it.

"This is a restricted channel," a voice replied. "Identify yourself. Over."

"My name is Aisha Bolland. We're in a forest just south of Glenridding. We need help."

"This is Sergeant Smithy. Over," a new voice cut in.

"Thank God," she muttered. "Ross gave us this frequency before. Please, I have kids with me."

"Is Ross with you now?"

"No. I've not heard from them for hours."

"Ok. There's a village south of you called Hartsop. I have a patrol passing through there in an hour, but you need to get there now. They won't wait."

Aisha scanned the map. "We can make that. Thank you."

Cassim gestured to the girl. "She's too cold," he said.

Aisha took off her jacket and wrapped it around her. "Hey, sweetie," she smiled. "Don't worry we'll take care of you for a while. What's your name?"

"...Luna Hague," the girl whispered.

42

James pulled his brother down the hill towards the shore.

"... Bowness might be a trap," Ross muttered.

"Shh," James spotted three figures creeping towards them from the lake, so the siblings dived into a ditch behind a fallen log and watched through the foliage. As the shapes passed, James realised that they were the same creatures with guns from the boat that followed them there. He held his breath until they were out of sight. James and Ross crawled out of the ditch, clambered down the slope and reached the treeline at the lake's edge.

From the shadows, they glimpsed Madeline sitting inside the creatures' moored speedboat. They got closer and saw that she was next to an infected guard who was holding a rifle.

"Please," she muttered. "I want to speak to my daughter."

"Shut up," the creature responded.

"But I did everything you asked me to? She's just a kid."

"Charles said we don't do anything until those brothers are dead. You know our deal."

"Fucking bitch..." Ross whispered. "She's working for them."

"We've got to get that boat," James quietly replied.

Ross snatched the pistol from his brother. "I'm a better shot than you."

"No. You're too dazed."

Ross glared back at James.

"... Fine," James hushed. "Just give me a sec. Don't hit Maddie."

James left Ross and crept further up the treeline. Once he was in position, he shouted out. The creature in the boat turned and aimed is rifle at the sound. Ross blasted at the beast, and it fell backwards, dropping its rifle and splashing into the water. Ross charged out of the treeline firing. Madeline cowered in the boat.

James scooped up a rock and sprinted towards her. "Don't fucking move," he said.

The brothers climbed into the boat. Ross picked up the rifle and aimed it at the still thrashing creature, who had black gunk oozing from the bullet holes in its body into the water.

"You bastards!" It bellowed. "You're both dead!"

"Fuck, these things are tough..." Ross grunted.

James started the boat's engine. The brothers sped away with Madeline in the vehicle.

43

James halted the boat in the middle of the lake.

Ross pointed his gun at Madeline. "Talk..." he grunted. "Or I swear you're going overboard."

"Shoot me," Madeline stuttered.

"Aisha and Cassim are dead," James interrupted. "My parents too. Charles murdered them!"

Madeline began to weep.

"Enough of that shit," Ross scolded.

"I'm sorry, Jim. Please –" she wailed.

"Charles has your daughter, doesn't he?" James cut in.

"He said he'd kill her if I didn't play along!"

"Tell us everything," Ross demanded. "Or I promise you won't see her again."

"I can't..." Madeline replied. Ross clicked the hammer back on his pistol and aimed it at her head.

Madeline wiped her eyes. "... We were at the GP Practice tonight, before you arrived," she muttered. "When those things attacked us, Ivy and the soldiers fled, but I stayed with my little girl and hid."

"Where did Ivy go to?" James asked.

Madeline shrugged. "When it was quiet, I wanted to leave with my daughter... But that's when Charles arrived."

"How the hell did Charles know to go there?" Ross queried.

"You two idiots told him," she said. "Hyland radioed your conversation to Charles when you picked him up, and he got there first... He asked me if I knew you two... Your family."

"You sold us out." Ross grumbled.

"He had my little Luna!" Madeline snapped. "You would have done the same thing. I saw you murder Hyland right in front of me!"

"What else did you tell him?" James butt in.

"Nothing! He tried to kill you at the GP Practice. Then those soldiers rescued you –"

"But then you show up at the hotel later telling us that Ivy's at Belle Ilse," James asserted.

"Fuck..." Madeline hesitated. "... Charles had a bunch of army radios. He overheard they were going to bomb Belle Isle. If Hyland and those things couldn't kill you at the hotel... I was supposed to sneak in and take you there –"

"So, you handed yourself in as a refugee to lure us out?" Ross interjected. "You might as well have shot us yourself."

"What's Charles planning at Bowness?" James asked.

"What?" she replied.

"Don't play dumb, bitch," Ross snarled.

"I promise, I'm not lying! I don't even know why Charles wants you so badly... I'm sorry, James. But I had to save my daughter."

Furious, James restarted the boat's engine.

"... Keep an eye on her, Ross," he mumbled.

44

James and Ross sat in the boat and surveyed Bowness' pier a hundred meters away. Madeline was slumped next to them with her hands tied. The brothers overheard faint screams in the distance, but the dock ahead of them was still and dead.

"Please let me go," Madeline whimpered. "If Charles sees me with you –"

"Shut your fucking mouth," Ross pressed his pistol into her ribs.

"There's not as much movement here as there was back at Ambleside," James muttered.

"I still think it's a bloody trap," Ross replied. "Those notes from the lab tell us anything useful?"

James read from the laminated papers in his hand. "The creatures are vulnerable to 'extreme changes in temperature'".

"So, no." Ross grunted.

James turned on the boat's engine and slowly drifted to shore. Once they were there, the brothers climbed out with Madeline and crept deeper into the town.

"Don't make a damn sound, you hear?" Ross whispered to Madeline.

The brothers and Madeline inched up the main road, lined by abandoned cars and broken glass. They reached a small restaurant by a cobbled alleyway. As they turned into a side street, a squad of soldiers leapt out from an alcove in front of them with their rifles raised.

"Drop the fucking guns!" one of them called out.

James and Ross slowly dropped their weapons and lay down next to Madeline. The soldiers frisked them and jammed thermometers into their ears. Then they hoisted Ross to his feet.

"Sir," one of them gestured for their sergeant to come over. The Sergeant, who was holding a piece of paper, approached Ross. He compared him with the portrait of Ross printed on it.

"Private fucking Bolland," the Sergeant said. "That means this other prick must be his brother."

Ross lunged towards the Sergeant, but the other soldiers held him back.

"Ross, no –!" James called.

"Shut up!" the Sergeant interrupted. "You boys are in a world of shit for what you pulled at the hotel."

"We didn't do anything," Ross growled.

The Sergeant stepped away and spoke into his radio, "Delta Four One to command. Hostile suspects James and Ross Bolland have been identified and secured in sector three five. We're on our way to you. Over."

The soldiers handcuffed James and Madeline and fastened Ross's arms behind his back. The squad dragged them away into a dark side street.

45

Charles stood on the cliffs with his men and scanned down at Bowness through binoculars. Most of the town was abandoned, but he saw that the soldiers had secured a small quarter of it and formed a perimeter as a base. Snipers guarded it from rooftops, and they'd sealed off the major access points in the streets using vehicles.

Charles spotted Madeline and the brothers being hauled by a squad towards the perimeter's main entryway. The soldiers manning it waved them through, and the brothers and Maddie were brought towards an old police station.

A creature approached Charles and handed him a C4 detonator. "The bomb's ready," he said. "Just flick the switch."

Charles grabbed his radio. "Van team. Report."

Charles looked through the binoculars to the deserted part of town. He saw his men guarding a van near a large, open sewer pipe. The vehicle shook violently.

"Ready and waiting," one of his men radioed back. "Our prisoners are very hungry."

Charles' heart raced. Finally, Penny was going to be avenged.

46

Aisha, Cassim and Luna shuffled out of the military vehicle with the other civilians into the Bowness base. The streets were a flurry of medical tents, shouting soldiers and distraught refugees. Aisha gripped the children close.

To her right, she noticed that the sergeant she'd travelled with was speaking with another sergeant. This new sergeant's uniform label read "Smithy", so she grabbed the kids and approached him.

"Excuse me, Sergeant Smithy?" she interrupted. "I'm Aisha Bolland. Thank you so much for your help."

"It's alright, ma'am," he responded.

"Have you heard anything about James or Ross? Please."

Smithy led Aisha and the children away to the doorway of a closed café. "Look, it's complicated," he whispered. "But they're ok."

"Thank God. Where are they?"

"I can't say much. They're here on the base and safe."

"They're here?!" Aisha gasped. "Are they hurt?"

"No, but they're in trouble."

"What do you mean?"

"It's classified, I'm sorry. But I thought you should know." Smithy tried to leave, but Aisha yanked him back.

"Ross' parents both died tonight," she pressed. "Those things nearly killed us as well –"

"Yeah? Well, my men are dead too!" Smithy cut in. "And those arseholes in command think Ross and your husband did it."

"What?!" Aisha hushed. "That's insane."

"It's a bloody mess... Your husband and Ross are locked up in the cells now."

"How? Can't you do anything? Surely you know they're innocent?"

"It doesn't matter what I think," Smithy recomposed himself, and glanced to see if anyone was watching. "They've got to be tried when this shit's all over."

"But what proof do they have? You know Ross wouldn't murder his own friends, and James doesn't know how to kill anyone."

"It's out of my hands."

"Ross said you would help us if we were ever in trouble. Was he wrong?"

"I've got bigger shit to deal with right now!" Smithy snapped. "I'll help Bolland prove his innocence once this nightmare's all over. Believe it or not, they're much safer in that cell than we are out here."

Smithy stormed off and left Aisha and the children in the doorway.

Aisha hugged her son. "Don't worry, Cas," she muttered. "Your dad's just fine."

47

James was slumped in the corner of his dark, concrete cell and listened to the sounds of Madeline sobbing through the walls in the next lock-up. He didn't know where his brother was. He kept thinking how stupid he'd been to leave his family. How Charles probably killed them. How he'd never see his parents, his wife, and his little boy again, and it was all his fault. Why was all this happening?

Shouting and gunshots erupted from outside. A huge explosion rattled the building and James scrambled to his feet. He jumped onto his bunk and strained to see out of the small, barred window at the top of the wall.

"Maddie!" he shouted. "Look out your window. Tell me what you see?"

Outside, he glimpsed a burning police car, and wounded people around it. Behind it, was a hole in the perimeter barricade. It looked like the car had smashed through it. Soldiers fired up at the hill beyond the perimeter.

"My God..." he heard Madeline say.

"Shit..." James muttered. If this attack got any closer, they'd be lambs for the slaughter.

48

Charles strode into the sewer chamber. Five other infected men were planting a C4 charge on the manhole cover above.

"Car team, report," Charles barked into his walkie-talkie.

"We're taking heavy fire," a harsh voice responded over the line. "We've drawn the soldiers away!"

One of the creatures handed Charles the detonator. "Ready when you are."

They all took cover behind the adjoining alcove. Charles pressed the detonator, and a pounding blast threw debris and dust everywhere. He glanced out and saw the entire town of Bowness above him.

"Release the prisoners," Charles ordered over the radio.

A rabble of mindless infected sprinted through the sewer passage and up towards the blast site. They scrambled up the pile of bricks and out into the town above, drawn by the scent of fresh meat.

"Move," Charles said to his men. He cocked his rifle, and they followed him up into the town. Time to finish this.

49

James' cell door flung open and Smithy, glazed in sweat and holding a rifle, strode in. Ross barged in after him and hauled James out into the hallway.

"Come on," Ross barked. "We're leaving."

"The hell is going on?!" James asked.

"The base has fallen," Smithy said. "I can't let you guys stay here and die."

"Aisha's alive, Jim," Ross interrupted. "Cassim too!"

"Where?!" James shouted.

"At a clock tower. A mile outside the perimeter."

"I evacuated them once this shit all started," Smithy interjected. "Told them to head there and to wait for you."

"You're just going to let us go?" James queried. "After what we did at the hotel?"

"You two didn't kill my boys," Smithy stated. "Don't make me regret trusting Aisha on this".

"Everyone's out there fighting those things," Ross cut in. "We've got to go."

Madeline banged on the inside of her cell door. "Don't leave me in here, you arseholes!" she cried.

James considered leaving her behind. He couldn't do it. The brothers unlocked her cell and pulled Madeline out.

"One more thing," Smithy continued. "Got a transmission from the comms room. A bunch of doctors are holding up in St Cuthbert's Church west of here. No idea if your sister's there –"

"It's a start," Ross said.

"Thank you," James told Smithy.

"Don't thank me," Smithy replied. "I was never here to help you escape. Just get your arses out of this base and don't look back."

Smithy led the brothers and Madeline towards the rear exit. He opened the door. Outside, rabid infected were attacking soldiers and civilians.

"Follow me!" Smithy barked at the brothers. They barged through the crowd. A gang of infected launched at them, but Smithy blasted the creatures. There were so many infected here, James thought. How quickly does this virus spread?!

They reached an alleyway with a fire escape at the end. It led up onto the roof of a one-story garage. Smithy gunned down the creatures that were following them, then charged up the staircase. "This way!" he bellowed. James and Madeline went after him.

Before Ross could catch up, a steel door in the alley burst open in front of him. Two infected scrambled out and lunged at him. James spun and saw that his brother was cut off.

Ross glanced up at James for a split-second. Then he turned and ran back out of the alley and into the crowd. The creatures loped after him.

He was leading them away, James realised. "Ross!" he called. "No-!" He went to move down the stairs, but Smithy yanked him back.

"Get to your wife and child!" Smithy grunted. He thrust a pistol into James' hand. "They need you! There's a way out off this roof." Smithy cocked his rifle. "I'll get Ross. We'll regroup at the clock tower. Follow the Lake Road north!" Smithy rushed down the stairs and disappeared into the chaos below.

James didn't want to leave his brother behind. But Madeline pulled on him. James moved with her onto the garage roof.

James glanced over the roof's edge. The hastily made perimeter wall was a twelve-foot drop below. The town of Bowness was quiet and black beyond it. He lowered himself down then helped Madeline descend. James gripped Madeline's arm, clenched the pistol, and they sprinted away.

The cries and gunshots echoed on the night wind behind him. He hoped to Christ Ross was alright.

50

James and Madeline shambled up the hilly lane out of town. They passed abandoned bed-and-breakfasts and cottages, and the mountains loomed in the distance ahead. James' lungs burned as he struggled up the final incline.

At the top, he spotted the clock tower. It stood in the centre of a cobbled, village square, surrounded by dark and empty buildings. There was no movement. Terrified, James wondered if he'd been too late. Had something already gotten to Aisha and his son?

A figure clambered out of a pub to his left. James raised his pistol. The figure brandished a meat cleaver and had black, bushy hair. It was Aisha.

"Jim...?" she asked meekly.

"Aisha!" James cried. The couple rushed together and embraced. James clasped her tightly in his arms. He promised himself he'd never leave her again. "I thought I'd lost you," he whispered.

"I'm so sorry," she muttered. "For everything –"

"No," James interrupted. "I'm sorry." He kissed her.

Cassim dashed out of the pub. "Dad!"

"Cassim!" James scooped his son up and squeezed him tight. "My special boy. I'm so glad you're alright –"

"Luna!" Madeline hollered.

James and Aisha turned. Madeline rushed to a little girl, who was emerging from the pub behind Aisha. She hugged the child. "Are you alright?" Madeline blustered. "How-?!" What happened?"

The little girl pointed to Aisha.

"You... saved her?" Madeline asked Aisha.

Aisha nodded.

"Thank you," Madeline muttered. "Thank you so much..."

51

James and Aisha sat together inside the pub and looked out of the bay window at the village square. Cassim was asleep at one of the tables behind them. Madeline whispered to Luna at the back of the pub.

"St Cuthbert's Church..." Aisha muttered. "You really think Ivy's there?"

James didn't reply. He was still thinking about what Aisha and Cassim had been through, and what she'd just told him about his parents. How Charles had brutally tracked them down and murdered them. Who was this Gail that infiltrated his family? Why was she working with these creatures? None of this made any sense.

James peeked back at Madeline. He still hated her for trying to lead him and Ross to their deaths. But, deep down, he understood why she did it. If Charles had kidnapped his son, he'd have done anything too. He hadn't decided what to do about her yet.

The fighting noises had died down from Bowness. James didn't know whether to wait longer or try to take his family to St Cuthbert's Church.

A figure waddled up the lane towards the clock tower. His movements were slow and jerky. James stood and clicked the hammer back on his pistol.

"Jim –" Aisha cautioned, gripping his arm. Madeline and Luna sat upright, alert.

"It's alright," James replied.

The figure staggered over to the clock tower then slumped down at its base. James strode out to meet the figure. As he got closer, he saw it was Ross. Ross was shaking, glazed in sweat, and had blood spattered on his boots. He glanced up at James. His eyes were teary and vacant.

"...Ross?" James queried.

"Smithy's dead..." Ross whimpered.

James held his brother. Ross began to weep.

"He got me out..." Ross went on. "Those things... They fucking ate him..."

"Shh" James stroked his brother's back. He glanced back at Aisha and waved that it was safe. "I'm sorry, Ross..." he muttered. "I'm so sorry."

52

James crept up the dark, woodland path with his pistol raised. Aisha and Cassim followed him with a map, and Madeline and Luna trailed behind them. Ross guarded their rear. The early morning sky was brightening, and a dull fog hung between the trees.

James spotted a steeple jutting from the foliage ahead. He crested the hill with his family. In a clearing before them, James saw a tall, gothic church with a sign that read "St Cuthbert's". The stained-glass windows were boarded up, and corpses lay on the carpark outside.

A dishevelled soldier rushed out from the back of the building, followed by two armed civilians who pointed their rifles at James.

"Stop!" the soldier barked. "Drop the gun!"

James lowered his pistol to the ground and raised his hands. "Is Dr Ivy Bolland here?" James asked.

"Please," Aisha added. "We're her family –"

"Shut up," the soldier snapped.

"Corporal!" a woman's stern voice interrupted.

James turned to see that the church's oak doors were now open. A small woman with bedraggled hair and a blood-stained shirt poked her head outside. It was Ivy.

"It's alright," Ivy ordered the soldier. "Let them in."

"They might be bitten," the Corporal grunted.

"They'll die out here if there's another attack. I'll check them inside."

The Corporal glowered at James and lowered his gun. "Second squad," he grumbled to his civilian comrades. "Back to the rooftop. Move."

The soldier and his squad disappeared behind the church. James scanned the building again, and saw that a sniper was watching them from the tower.

Ivy gestured for James to come inside.

James scooped up his pistol. He led Aisha, Cassim, Madeline, Luna, and Ross to the doorway. Ivy hugged each one as they entered, but she stopped Madeline.

"Maddie?!" Ivy asked. "... My God. Are you alright?"

Madeline didn't say a word. She slipped inside with Luna.

James embraced Ivy, then closed the door behind them all.

The interior of the church was dimly lit with camping lights, and James' eyes struggled to adjust to the darkness. In the main hall, the pews were lined up like a hospital ward and several bloodied patients lay on them. Two doctors flitted between each bed. The air stunk like sweat and chemicals.

"The hell are you doing here, Jim?" Ivy muttered.

"It's complicated," James replied.

"Where's mum and dad?"

James hesitated. He didn't have the heart to tell her. But then he saw her eyes darken, and he knew that Ivy had worked it out on her own.

"What happened here?" James asked.

"When we left Acorn Practice," Ivy said, "a few of those things chased us. Anyone who could fight, did. We boarded ourselves up in here to wait for evac –"

"Jim!" Aisha hushed. She gestured for James to come to her.

"That's her," Aisha whispered and pointed into the church's main hall. "That's Gail."

James followed the line of Aisha's finger and looked past the make-shift hospital ward. At the front of the church, by the altar, stood a small group of people. A blonde-haired woman in a suit was amongst them.

"Are you sure?" James queried.

The blonde woman glanced back at James and Aisha. Her eyes widened. She dashed towards a side exit.

"Stop her!" Aisha bellowed. "She's working with the infected!"

A bandaged soldier near the blonde woman tackled her and pinned her to the ground. Aisha pushed her way through the doctors in the main hall. James and Ross followed.

Looks like our reunion will have to wait, James thought. A cold fear gripped his stomach.

53

James, Ross, Aisha, and Ivy watched as two soldiers interrogated the blonde woman at a table at the other end of the room.

"Her name is Gail," Ivy muttered. "The other patients confirmed it. She came as a refugee about an hour ago."

The Corporal from outside strode to Ivy. James noted that his nametag read "Wilcox".

"We found this on her," Wilcox grumbled and held up a small radio. "It's tuned to a frequency that isn't ours. She took it from our supplies."

"She's radioing Charles," Aisha interrupted.

"Who?"

"The thing that killed our parents, sir," Ross said.

"Slow down," Wilcox replied. "Tell me exactly what this woman did."

"She came to our home earlier tonight looking for help," Aisha explained. "We let her in, she... Led those things right to us."

James saw that Aisha was struggling to relive the trauma of what happened and was trying to not let it show. He held her hand.

Aisha went on. "That woman helped those monsters kill my mother and father-in-law."

"You sure that's her?" Wilcox pointed at Gail.

Aisha nodded.

"Corporal," James butt in, "some of these infected are smart. They have people working with them."

"Surely, you've heard some reports?" Ross queried.

"I've heard nothing about this 'Charles'," Wilcox murmured.

"It sounds far-fetched," Ivy said to the Corporal, "but Aisha wouldn't lie. If Gail really did contact the infected, then we're all in danger here."

James glared at Gail. She just stared at the floor. He felt a white-hot rage boiling inside of him. If Aisha was right, then this woman was responsible for the deaths of his parents. She had led the infected to Nan's house and nearly killed Aisha and his son. She was working for Charles.

"I'll speak to her," James insisted.

"No," Wilcox replied.

"Sir, we need intel," Ross chimed in. "If there's an assault coming –"

"What makes you think he can get answers out of her if there is?" Wilcox pointed at James.

"Because we've had to kill a few of her friends to get here alive," James asserted. "Gail wants us dead. If you sit me down in front of her, she could crack."

"We're out of time, Corporal," Ivy stressed. "Our patients won't survive another attack. We have to try something."

"Fuck..." Wilcox paced. He turned to James. "You've got two minutes. My boys will supervise. Hand me your sidearm. You are not to touch her, understand?"

Wilcox held his hand out. James reluctantly relinquished the pistol.

"Then you three are joining me for the defence of this place," Wilcox pointed at James, Ross, and Aisha. He turned to Ivy. "You too, doctor."

Wilcox strode to the two men guarding Gail. He muttered to them.

Taking a breath, James shared a concerned look with his wife, his sister, and his brother. Two minutes was not a lot of time. But all their lives were at stake.

James sat down in front of Gail. Wilcox and the two soldiers moved aside and watched.

"...Charles sent you here to spy on us," James said as calmly as he could. "But he isn't coming for you."

Gail did not move.

"You murdered my parents," he sneered. "Tried to kill my wife. My son... I took a lot of pleasure in shooting some of your mates."

Gail looked at James with a hard, venomous stare. "Fuck you," she mumbled.

"They were all mutant freaks," James growled. "They deserved to be put down. Hyland too –"

Gail leapt to her feet and punched the table. "You monster!" she yelled. "Child killer!"

The two soldiers rushed at her. One shoved her back down into the chair and held her in place. She continued, "you think because they're infected, they're not people?!"

"The hell you talking about?" James asked.

"My little girl, Penny! You ran her down and left her to die!"

James didn't understand. But then he remembered. Earlier tonight, once he'd snuck past the police barricade, he hit a creature in his truck and killed her. That couldn't be what Gail was talking about?

"Charles is going to find you," Gail continued. Tears streamed from her eyes, but she didn't blink, and she didn't waver. "He's going to rip you all to pieces."

"Who is he?" James demanded.

"You seriously don't know? He was there when you killed her. He's Penny's father!"

James recalled that there was a figure that tried to attack them when he and Ross got out of their vehicle to help the infected girl.

"And Hyland was my damn brother, you cunt," Gail grunted.

"What's Charles planning?" James commanded.

"You'll find out soon enough. Your soldier friends weren't the only ones who got Ivy's SOS."

One of the soldiers guarding Gail put a finger to his ear-mic. "We've got movement," he announced. "Fifty meters south."

"You're all dead men," Gail grinned. "You'll be with your parents soon."

54

Charles and his men hid in the treeline and looked down at St Cuthbert's Church in the clearing below. Through his binoculars, Charles spotted a sniper in the tower. He glimpsed hurried, shadowy movements behind the barricaded windows. Something had spooked the soldiers inside.

"Charles," a familiar voice crackled over his radio. Charles immediately recognised it as James.

"We've got Gail hostage in here," James continued. "We know about your plan. If you fire on us, you'll be killing her too. You have been warned."

Charles' men glanced at him nervously. "...What do we do?" one of them asked.

Charles felt guilty. He never stopped loving Gail, even after the divorce. But he knew there was a chance that she'd never leave that church alive if her cover was blown. Just like when he told her to sneak past the police cordon to infiltrate the brothers' house earlier that night.

He hoped Penny would forgive him for what he was about to do.

Charles spoke through his second radio. "Group Two. Open fire."

"But Charles –" one of the infected next to him protested.

"We stick to the plan!" Charles barked.

A hail of gunfire erupted from the treeline at the opposite side of the clearing. Bullets pounded the church, and the sniper in the tower dove for cover. Charles saw the silhouettes guarding the windows dash away. They blasted up at the incoming fire at the far side of the church.

Charles grabbed the vodka bottle to his left and stuffed a rag into the top. "Move!" Charles yelled. He gripped his lighter and dashed out of the treeline with his men.

***

Inside the church, James, Ross, Wilcox, and some soldiers took cover by the west windows and blasted up at their attackers. To his right, Aisha shielded Cassim and Luna with her body and gripped a pistol tight.

Behind him, Ivy, Madeline, and the doctors frantically dragged their patients behind the stone pillars, as glass shards and ricochets skimmed past them. A wounded civilian guarded Gail with a knife.

James heard a cry to his left. He saw a soldier drop to the floor and clutch a gaping hole in his neck as blood spurted out. A burst of rifle fire cut through the windows above him and a doctor and two patients behind him dropped dead.

Aisha put the two children behind cover and dashed out to relieve Ivy and Madeline.

"Aisha!" James called to her.

Aisha grabbed a patient under his arms and dragged him to safety. In that moment, James was both terrified for her, and loved her.

The windows at the east side of the church smashed open and the barricades burst into flames. Another firebomb flew in and smashed against the confessional. The fire spread into the rafters. James realised that Charles had deliberately drawn them to one side of the church, so he could cook them from behind.

As the flames surged and engulfed the ceiling, Gail elbowed her captor. He doubled over, and she dashed away towards the door. James raised his pistol at her, but she was already outside.

James cursed, but he was thankful that he didn't have time to gun Gail down in cold blood.

James felt the heat on his skin.

"Put those flames out!" Wilcox barked to his men. But James knew it was too late. He had to get everyone out. Now.

***

Charles squatted behind a rock and blasted at the burning church. Smoke billowed out of the windows as orange licks of flame swept over the roof. The warmth pressed against his chitinous skin.

His men had surrounded the building and were firing inside.

Charles spotted a figure running in the open to his right. He saw it was Gail. But it was too late.

An infected cut her in half with a burst of gunfire, and she tumbled into the grass.

"No!" Charles roared. He stood, dropped his weapon, and dashed over to her. He knelt over Gail's lifeless body. She was pale and blood leaked from her stomach... She looked just like Penny.

...This was all his fault.

55

James squinted through the acrid smoke, as the flames around him burned brighter. A bullet sliced through Wilcox's thigh. He fell, cursing, and James and Ivy scrambled to him.

James pressed his hands onto Wilcox' wound, while Ivy placed a torniquet on his leg.

"Corporal," Ivy shouted. "We have to use the undercroft. It's our only chance!"

"The what?" James asked.

"...Secret passage..." Wilcox grunted. "Under the church..."

Ivy wrapped Wilcox's leg in a crude bandage. She pointed to a narrow, stone archway behind the pulpit. "It leads out into the graveyard," she explained. "We can unlock it."

"It's suicide!" Wilcox interrupted "...There's no cover out there. Those bastards will pick us off."

"Better than roasting to death in here," James remarked.

He gestured for Ross to come over. Ross dashed to Wilcox, looped the Corporal's arm over his shoulder, and hoisted him to his feet.

"Gather everyone," James ordered Ross and Ivy. "We're heading downstairs."

James picked Cassim and Luna up.

"It's ok, Cas," James whispered. "Daddy's got you."

James ran over to Aisha and Madeline and handed the children to them. "We're leaving." James barked. "Back exit. Move."

James, Aisha, and Madeline corralled the patients towards the archway.

Ross, Ivy, and Wilcox were already at the crypt's entrance pushing wounded soldiers and civilians into the passage. Aisha, Madeline, and the children hurried the patients inside and followed.

James took one last look at the church. Corpses lay amongst the ravaging flames.

"... My boys!" Wilcox cried, looking at the bodies. "No!"

Ross dragged a thrashing Wilcox into the passage. Ivy and James followed, then sealed the door behind them.

In the pitch darkness, the air thick with smoke, James crept down the stone steps with Ivy. Grunts of pain and panicked murmuring echoed from below.

"The Corporal's right," Ivy mumbled. "It's a hundred yards from the tunnel's exit to the treeline... Not all of us will make it."

"We've got to try." James said.

James entered a stone chamber, lit only by the faint torches of soldiers. Clusters of patients and civilians huddled together around tombs. James pushed his way through the crowd towards Aisha and Cassim.

"You ok?" James asked.

Aisha nodded. "You?"

James held them. "I love you both... No matter what."

Ivy unlocked a steel gate at the far side of the room.

The soldier with her poked her head into the tunnel. "It's clear!" she called. "Everyone move. Quiet-like. Once you're outside, keep running to the trees and don't stop."

James moved with Aisha and Cassim towards the gate. One by one, he helped everyone into the tunnel. Once the crowd was inside, James and Ivy followed.

They rushed down the narrow, stone passage but spotted that the evacuees had stopped near the end.

"What's the fucking hold up?!" a voice hushed.

"There's a chain blocking the gate!" someone replied. "We're trapped!"

"Shoot that bloody chain!" Ross grumbled. "Now, or we all die!"

56

A gunshot rang out, and Charles looked up. He realised that he'd been cradling Gail's body for a few minutes. His men were now standing around the church in the open as it burned. No gunfire was coming from inside.

An infected rushed to Charles. "It sounded like it came from the graveyard!" He pointed to a small stone path that led up over the knoll.

Charles expected the brothers to keep fighting until the end. It seemed too convenient that no one tried to flee the building, and that the shooting from inside suddenly stopped. Perhaps that far-off gunshot was someone coming to flank him?

Charles gestured to three infected. "You three, stay," he bellowed. "Everyone else, with me."

Charles marched with his remaining men towards the top of the knoll. His rotten skin felt hard and itchy by the fire. But with every step away, it became harder to breathe, like his ribs were contracting. His skin felt thinner, more brittle, and an ice-chill penetrated his bones. By the time they reached the top, Charles and his men were shivering and gasping for air.

"... The hell is happening to us?!" one of them cried.

Charles surveyed the graveyard below. He glimpsed some figures scrambling out of a tomb at the far side towards the trees, and spotted James.

"There!" Charles yelled. He bolted forward, but a searing pain flashed in his leg, and he fell. He saw an agonising pool of black ooze dripping from his leg.

His men writhed on the ground too, tearing new wounds in their paper-thin skin each time they moved. The fuck was going on?

57

James and Ivy sprinted with the remaining patients towards the treeline. Ross, Wilcox, Aisha, Cassim, and some soldiers were already there and were pushing the evacuees deeper into the forest.

"Is this everyone?" James shouted.

"I think so," Aisha replied. "Maddie and Luna took off running with the others."

"The fuck are the infected doing?" Ross asked. He pointed to the far side of the graveyard.

James looked. A gang of creatures were stumbling down the hill, bleeding profusely, and struggling to stand. Their grunts of pain echoed on the wind. James saw the flames of the church surging behind them.

"...Extreme changes in temperature..." James mumbled. He turned to Ross. "We have to go back."

"What?" Ross responded.

"The infected are weak now. We can stop them here."

"What are you talking about?" Aisha stepped forward.

James gestured to the fire on the horizon. "That heat has softened them up. Those monsters can't take the drop to normal temperature. We can pump them full of holes."

"How the hell do you know all this?" Wilcox growled.

"I just do," James snapped. He didn't want to reveal that he'd stolen notes from the military lab these creatures had come from.

"Jim, we can leave now," Aisha interjected. "Take this chance to escape."

James held Aisha. "They tried to kill you and Cassim…" He turned to the soldiers. "They murdered my parents and your squad mates. Are we just going to let them get away with it?!"

"It's a huge risk," Ross whispered to James. "We don't know if those scientist's notes were right."

"Charles has followed us all night," James asserted. "We won't be safe until he's dead." He turned to Ivy. "Take Aisha, Cassim, and Wilcox down the ravine. If we don't meet you in five minutes, keep going."

"Fuck that," Wilcox cut in. "I'm staying –"

"James, please," Aisha held her husband's hand. "Don't do this."

James gazed into her terrified, maple eyes for perhaps the last time. "…I'm sorry" he muttered. "But I have to. For the family…" James hugged her and Cassim. "Now go."

James turned to Ross and the soldiers. "The rest of you – Let's go put the dead back in their graves."

James sprinted out of the treeline with Ross and the soldiers, whilst Ivy dragged Wilcox, Aisha, and Cassim away.

Ahead, James overheard a terrified infected calling his comrades to attention. The creatures scrambled for cover and blasted at the soldiers. Bullets whizzed past James' head, as he dove behind a gravestone. Gunfire shredded the tombs around him and sent chunks of stone hurtling through the air.

James glanced to his left and saw the soldiers advancing cover-to-cover on the creatures. They riddled two infected with rifle-bursts, but one soldier caught a bullet in the chest.

James moved to help them, but Ross held him back.

"Let's flank them," Ross yelled. He pointed to their right, at an emptier part of the graveyard.

The brothers dashed through the headstones. Gunfire clattered past. James hit the deck, but Ross carried on, firing controlled shots at their attackers and drawing their fire.

James clambered to his feet and saw a wounded infected lurching toward them. James unloaded a full clip into its body.

Another infected spotted the brothers. He blasted at James. James leapt behind a tombstone and frantically tried to reload.

Ross leant out from behind a mausoleum. "Hey!" he called.

The creature turned. Ross shot out both his kneecaps. The beast dropped, groaning. James slapped the last magazine into his pistol, rolled out, and blew the creature's brains out.

Ross helped James to his feet. "You alright?" he asked.

"Yeah," James replied.

The brothers rushed through the remaining graves and emerged at the far side.

Fifty yards to his left, James spotted a pile of infected corpses. Charles' surviving men were desperately limping back up the knoll. James' soldiers were shooting them in the back and cheering, with some executing the infected as they tried to crawl.

"We did it..." James muttered. A wave of relief washed over his body.

"Fuck!" Ross yelped.

James spun. A wounded infected was wrestling with Ross. James aimed, but he couldn't get a clear shot.

The infected snatched Ross' gun. He dragged Ross close, used him as a shield, and pointed the weapon at Ross' throat.

"Shout for help, and I'll kill him," the creature snarled.

James recognised the voice. It was Charles. Charles' eyes burnt with fury as black ichor leaked from his wounds.

"Shoot the prick, Jim!" Ross cried. "It doesn't matter about me."

"Your brother's right," Charles smiled. "He's already dead."

An arachnoid appendage sprouted from Charles' back and ripped open Ross' shirt. James spotted a bite mark on his brother's torso, surrounded by blackened, necrotic flesh.

"Got bitten a few hours ago," Charles smirked. "He's infected. And I've already lost everything. You want to keep your family safe? Kill us both."

James' heart sank. Tears built up in his eyes.

"It's alright, Jim," Ross muttered. "...Do it."

James' hands began to shake as he took aim.

"...Bloody do it!" Ross ordered.

"Fuck..." James whispered... His finger slowly tightened on the trigger...

A gunshot rang out.

The back of Charles' head exploded, and Ross scrambled free.

James realised he hadn't fired. Diving for cover, he glanced to see where the shot had come from.

A figure stepped out from behind a tombstone holding a smoking gun... It was Ivy.

Aisha and Cassim darted out of the overgrowth behind Ivy and embraced James. "Dad!" Cassim shrieked.

"The hell-?" James whispered.

"Shh. It's alright, James," Aisha stroked his face. "You're safe now."

"We didn't want to leave you," Ivy grunted.

"But... Wilcox?" James murmured.

"He's back in the trees keeping watch," Ivy said.

"It's over," Aisha reiterated. "Those things are dead."

James gazed into Aisha's eyes. He remembered how much he loved her, how precious their son was, and how close he'd come to losing them. He felt awful for how he treated them.

"I'm so sorry..." James whispered, holding them tight. "For everything."

"No," Aisha replied. "I'm sorry. We all are."

James glanced at Ivy and Ross, and noted that this was the first time they'd all been together in a year... Only this time, without their parents...

James noticed that Ross was hiding his bite from the others. Ross and Aisha's drunken fling still hurt James. But he couldn't think about that now.

"Get ready to leave with the soldiers," James advised Aisha and Ivy. "I need to speak to Ross."

Ivy gave a worried glance to Ross.

"...Goodbye, Ross," Ivy said gravely. She gathered Aisha and Cassim and ferried them away towards the soldiers.

Ross slumped against a tombstone and coughed up black bile. His eyes were turning a sickly yellow.

"Those fuckers bit me when we got split up in Bowness..." Ross admitted. "Ivy didn't get a chance to check me over, before Charles attacked the church."

Ross reached for Charles' gun, but James snatched it away.

"Damn it, Jim," Ross protested. "I don't want to turn into one of those things."

"You're not going to," James replied.

"Fucking look at me. I'm a goner. Just put a bullet in me."

"I can find help."

"There's no help," Ross stressed. "Just do it. Please."

"Those scientists made this virus," James interrupted. "Maybe they have a cure?"

"I'm going to turn," Ross emphasised. "I'm going to lose my mind and hurt people. Maybe even our own family –"

"Just give me a few more hours, I promise," James demanded. "I'll go with these soldiers. I'll tell their leadership we have people lost in this forest. They'll come back and help us."

"Or put me in a body bag," Ross grunted.

"I can't lose you!" James shouted. "I just can't...Please. Let me help..."

Ross nodded.

"Hide somewhere safe," James added. "I'll be back in a few hours, ok?"

James started to leave.

"Jim," Ross called after him. "I'm sorry about what I did."

James stopped. He knew Ross was talking about his affair with Aisha.

"I know," James replied. "And it's alright... Stay safe."

James darted away towards his family. He knew it was a long shot, but he was going to save his brother.

58

Ross watched James, Aisha, Cassim, Ivy, Wilcox, and the soldiers disappear over the knoll. He breathed a sigh of relief.

He searched Charles' body for weapons, but there were none.

He dragged himself over to the infected corpses fifty yards away. The virus in his brain burnt like a hot scalpel, but he pushed on. Once he was there, he saw that the guns had been picked clean by the soldiers. He spotted a knife tucked into an infected cadaver's boot.

Ross snatched it and held the blade to his forearm. He knew James wouldn't get back in time. The top brass might still believe him to be the hotel bomber and imprison him. Ross just didn't want James to worry.

Ross made a promise to protect his family. Now he needed to protect them from himself.

"Sorry, Jim," Ross mumbled. He stabbed into his forearm. Searing pain jolted through him, but he pushed the knife in deeper and slashed along his veins to the wrist. Black pus and blood poured from the gaping wound.

Feeling faint, he gazed up at the morning sky. Had he done enough to redeem himself? Would his family forgive him for a lifetime of fuck ups? Will his parents be waiting for him on the other side?

That thought gave him hope... He held onto it, closed his eyes, and drifted away into blackness.